Skittle in the Middle

HarperCollins *Children's Books*

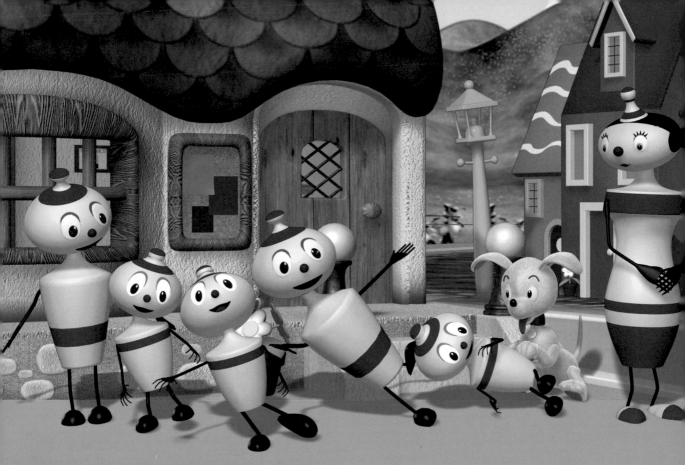

It was a beautiful day in Toyland and the Skittle family were playing fetch with Bumpy Dog.

"Come on, fetch the stick, Bumpy!" called Mrs Skittle.

"Woof woof!" barked Bumpy Dog, as he came bounding up and knocked over all of the Skittle children.

"Wheeee!" laughed the children as they fell. All skittles love to fall down!

"That was fun, mother," said the Skittle children. "What do we do now?"

"Well, children," replied Mrs Skittle, "why don't we go and visit Mr Wobbly Man? He's always good for a wobble-tumble."

Everyone was excited, apart from Skippy Skittle.

"Hurry, Skippy, it's your turn to stand in front!" the Skittle children told him.

"Maybe later. I'm a bit busy right now. Bye."

And with that, Skippy walked off.

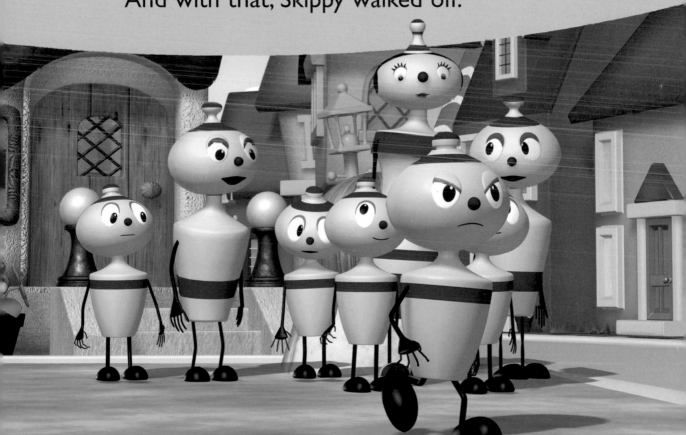

Skippy Skittle was in Toy Town when Clockwork
Clown came along.

"Hello, Skippy. Allow me," Clockwork
Clown said, as he knocked Skippy over.

Clockwork Clown chuckled as he walked
off, thinking he had done Skippy a favour.

"Whoa! Why does everyone think that all skittles want to do is fall dowwwwwn!" No sooner had Skippy Skittle picked himself up than he fell again as a bouncing ball knocked him over.

"Heh heh… that was a good bounce, Bouncy Ball," said Skippy, mustering all the enthusiasm he could.

Just then, Noddy drove up to Skippy Skittle in his little taxi.

"Hi, Skippy. How are you today?"

"Hi, Noddy," answered Skippy. "I'm okay."

"Just okay? Well, you'll feel better once I push you over!" offered Noddy.

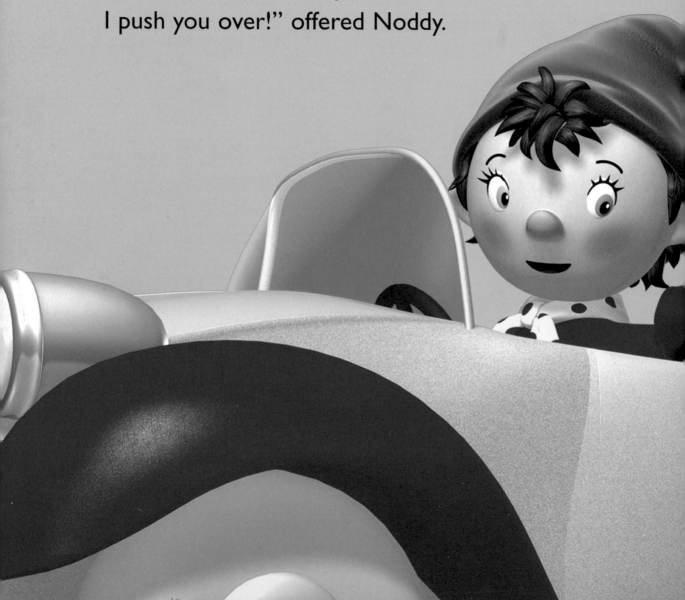

"No! I don't want to fall down!" cried Skippy, sadly.

"I thought all Skittles liked falling down better than anything, except for… hmm… well, better than **anything**!" said Noddy.

Skippy was confused.

"I do like falling down," he told Noddy.
"I mean, they do... I mean, why do all Skittles
have to do the same thing? Why can't they do
something different?"

"Like what?" asked Noddy. "Grow flowers?
Climb a tree? Watch birds?"

"Well," answered Skippy, "like baking
googleberry muffins. That's different to falling
down, isn't it?"

"It definitely is," Noddy assured him.
"You should try it!"

Noddy sang a song to cheer Skippy up.

Everybody's different
Different is okay
What makes us different
Changes every day
We might have different families
Or a different name
Everybody's different
That's how we're the same!

Skippy thought that his family would be cross with him if he told them he didn't want to fall down all the time.

"Just tell them, Skippy," Noddy urged. "They'll understand."

"I don't know about that, Noddy."

"Sure they will, Skippy. Come on!"

Off they went to find the rest of the Skittle family.

The Skittle family were lined up outside the police station.

"What are you doing, mother?" asked Skippy.

"Shh. Get in line, Skippy. You too, Noddy," instructed Mrs Skittle. "Alright, children, you know what to do."

Just then, Mr Plod came along. "What's the
problem here?" he asked.
The Skittles all whistled and hummed innocently.
    "Stop in the name of Plod!" cried Mr Plod,
and all the Skittles and Noddy fell down.
    "Good job, children! And Noddy!" said Mrs
Skittle, happily.

"This is no time for games, Mrs Skittle!" exclaimed
Mr Plod. "I'm busy with official police business."
The Skittle children all apologised to Mr Plod.

"What kind of business?" they asked.

"Er, well, um…" Mr Plod stuttered. "Dinah
Doll asked me to taste her freshly baked
googleberry muffins. I've got to hurry over before
they get cold!" he told them as he disappeared.

"Speaking of googleberry muffins… go ahead,
Skippy," urged Noddy.
    "I can't!" replied Skippy.
    "What's the matter, Skippy?" his mother asked.
    "Well, it's just that, um, I don't really feel like
toppling…"

Mrs Skittle feared the worst.

"What?! You're not bored with falling over are you?"

All of the Skittle children joined with Mrs Skittle to chorus, "A Skittle loves to fall, more than anything at all!"

"What I meant was, I don't really feel like toppling the same old way all the time," Skippy tried to explain.

"Well, why didn't you say so, Skippy?" Mrs Skittle asked, with a smile.

"Gather up every Skittle, children. We're about to take our biggest tumble ever, and it's guaranteed to make Skippy smile!" Mrs Skittle instructed.

The Skittle children all cheered.

Noddy leant into Skippy's ear. "You have got to learn to speak your mind, Skippy."

"I will tell them, Noddy… some day," Skippy replied.

"Come on, Skippy!" said Scooter and Shelly, taking Skippy by the hand.

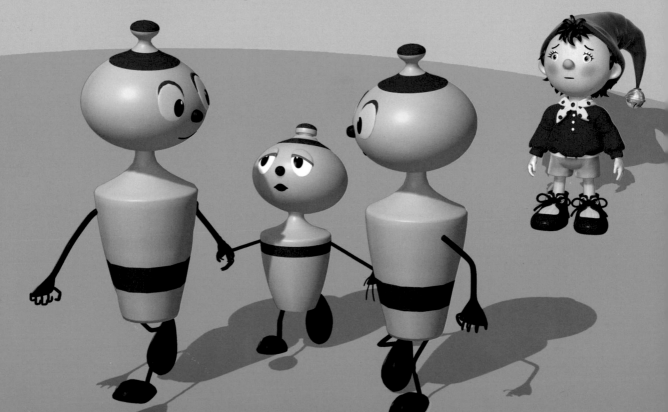

Mrs Skittle led her family out to the hills outside Toy Town. When they were all lined up, she called to Bumpy Dog.

"Here he comes! On your marks, get set ... **fall**!" cried Mrs Skittle.

One by one, all the skittles fell down.
"Wheeee!" they all cheered.

Back in Toy Town, Mr Plod bought himself
a googleberry muffin from Dinah Doll's stall.

"Here you are, Mr Plod. Freshly baked
muffins good enough to knock you off
your feet," smiled Dinah Doll.

"It takes more than a muffin to knock me
over, Dinah Doll!" laughed Mr Plod.

In Toy Town square, the Skittle family were lining
up for another tumble, this time with
Clockwork Clown.

"Are you sure you want to do this?"
Noddy asked Skippy.

"Every Skittle will be upset with me if I
don't!" worried Skippy.

Skippy Skittle did not fall. "Our family topple is ruined!" the other skittle children gasped.

"Oh dear!" cried Mrs Skittle. "What's wrong, darling?" she asked.

"Tell them what you told me, Skippy," Noddy said, firmly.

"What is it, Skippy? What's wrong?" Mrs Skittle
asked, urgently.

"I… um… I," Skippy started, nervously.
"I want to do something other than fall down all
the time."

"You do? Like what?" gasped Mrs Skittle.
"I want to bake some muffins!"

"Oh, no!" cried all the Skittle children. "Skippy doesn't want to fall down anymore!"

"No, no, I love to fall down, really. It's just..." Skippy faltered.

"It's just that it's okay to do more than one thing. Right, Mrs Skittle?" Noddy came to Skippy's rescue.

"Actually," thought Mrs Skittle, "I've always wanted to bake some muffins, too!"

"Come to think of it, I've always wanted to finish my own sentences. And fly a kite," added Scooter.

"And I'd like to learn to walk on my hands, like Clockwork Clown," said Shelly.

"You mean it's okay for me to bake some muffins, mother?" asked Skippy.

"I think it's a wonderful idea," Mrs Skittle agreed.

Skippy brought his muffins out for his friends and family to try.

"These googleberry muffins you baked are tasty, Skippy!" Mrs Skittle congratulated.

"I'll say," said Noddy. "Tasty, tasty, tasty!"

The other Skittle children were very excited
about the muffins, too. "Wheeee!" they chorused.
Skippy was much happier and thanked Noddy
for his help.

'You were right, Noddy," said Skippy. Learning to speak up for yourself is a good thing. I'm so happy that I could just, well… fall down!"